"Faster!" Sophia gasped as her dark curls blew out behind her. All thoughts disappeared from her head apart from the feeling of speed and Rainbow's warm back beneath her. This was like flying!

LOOK OUT FOR MORE
ADVENTURES AT

UNICORN ACADEMY

Sophia and Rainbow
Scarlett and Blaze
Ava and Star
Isabel and Cloud
Layla and Dancer
Olivia and Snowflake

★ ★ ★

UNICORN ✦ ACADEMY
Sophia and Rainbow

JULIE SYKES
illustrated by LUCY TRUMAN

A STEPPING STONE BOOK™

Random House 🏠 New York

Text copyright © 2018 by Julie Sykes and Linda Chapman
Cover art and interior illustrations copyright © 2018 by Lucy Truman

All rights reserved. Published in the United States by Random House Children's Books, a division of Penguin Random House LLC, New York. Originally published in paperback by Nosy Crow Ltd, London, in 2018.

Random House and the colophon are registered trademarks and A Stepping Stone Book and the colophon are trademarks of Penguin Random House LLC.

Visit us on the Web! rhcbooks.com

Educators and librarians, for a variety of teaching tools,
visit us at RHTeachersLibrarians.com

Library of Congress Cataloging-in-Publication Data
Names: Sykes, Julie, author. | Truman, Lucy, illustrator.
Title: Sophia and Rainbow / Julie Sykes; illustrated by Lucy Truman.
Description: First American edition. | New York: Random House, 2019. |
Series: Unicorn Academy ; #1 | Originally published in London by Nosy Crow
in 2018. | Summary: "After ten-year-old Sophia meets her unicorn, Rainbow, at
Lakeside Unicorn Academy, they're away on their first amazing adventure—they
must discover who is tampering with the lake that gives unicorns their magic!"
Identifiers: LCCN 2018027746 | ISBN 978-1-9848-5082-9 (paperback) |
ISBN 978-1-9848-5083-6 (hardcover library binding) |
ISBN 978-1-9848-5084-3 (ebook)
Subjects: | CYAC: Unicorns—Fiction. | Magic—Fiction. |
Boarding schools—Fiction. | Schools—Fiction.
Classification: LCC PZ7.S98325 So 2019 | DDC [Fic]—dc23

Printed in the United States of America
10 9 8 7 6 5 4 3 2 1
First American Edition

UNICORN ACADEMY

Sophia and Rainbow

CHAPTER 1

"We're almost at the school!" exclaimed Sophia, seeing a sign just ahead. The swirly gold writing on it said UNICORN ACADEMY beside a painting of a snow-white unicorn with a rainbow arching over its head. An arrow pointed up a long, tree-lined drive.

"Race you!" called Harry, Sophia's seven-year-old brother.

Sophia couldn't wait to see the school after five hours of riding, and she would have loved to gallop, but she slid from her shaggy gray pony's back and patted his neck fondly. "Sorry, Harry,

but Clover's tired. I'm not going to make him race."

Clover, who was old and couldn't go fast anymore, pushed his nose gratefully into Sophia's hair. Her wavy black curls hung over his muzzle like a droopy mustache. Sophia giggled, but there was a heavy weight in her stomach. Now that she was ten, she was thrilled to be old enough to attend Unicorn Academy and finally get a unicorn of her own. But she was really going to miss Clover!

"All right, sweetie?" asked her mom, trotting up alongside. Solitaire, her mom's unicorn, was fully grown and looked very elegant compared to short-legged Clover. "You're going to have a fantastic time here at the school, but I expect it feels quite strange at the moment. Remember to be polite and please try to think first before rushing into things."

Sophia grinned. "As if I'd do that, Mom!"

"Hmm," her mom said, raising her eyebrows.

Then her expression softened. "Remember that all the other girls and boys will probably be feeling as nervous as you. But it won't be long before you get to know each other."

"I am a little bit nervous about making friends," admitted Sophia, "but I'm more worried about Clover." She stroked Clover's neck. "Do you think he'll be okay without me?"

"He'll be fine," said her mom. "He's getting old, and he'll be happy having a quieter life. Harry and I will make sure he gets lots of cuddles. Don't worry about Clover. Just enjoy getting to know your own special unicorn, bonding and learning to work together to protect our island."

Sophia's heart swelled. She loved the thought of protecting Unicorn Island, their beautiful home. "I wonder what my unicorn will be like and what its magical power will be. I hope it can heal like Solitaire."

Each unicorn was born with its own special magical power. There were many different powers, and young unicorns usually found out what they could do in their first year at Unicorn Academy.

Sophia's mom leaned down to push a stray black curl out of Sophia's eyes. "I'm sure you'll love your unicorn, whatever power it has."

Sophia fell quiet as she climbed back onto Clover and rode him through the green tunnel of trees toward the school. She really wanted her unicorn to be able to heal. With healing magic, maybe she could take away some of Clover's aches and pains.

The tunnel ended, and Sophia rode Clover out into the pale January sunlight. Excitement rushed

inside her as she stared at the enormous building of marble and glass with a fountain sparkling in front of it. She'd dreamed of this moment for years.

"It's beautiful." She could hardly tear her eyes away from the majestic towers of the school and the perfectly kept gardens surrounding it that were filled with plants and flowers, even in winter. In the distance, the multicolored, magical water of the famous Sparkle Lake glittered in the sunshine.

"I wish I was old enough to come here," said Harry longingly.

Girls and boys were rushing in all directions. Teachers called out instructions. A group of girls stood together at the bottom of the steps that swept up to the school's front door. They looked like they'd just arrived. Sophia took a deep breath. This was it. Time to say goodbye to Clover and her family! She wrapped her arms around Clover's

neck, burying her face and tears in his soft mane.

"Goodbye, Clover darling. Have a nice rest grazing in the field."

Mom touched her arm. "Shall I walk you over to the others?"

"No, I'll be fine." Sophia dried her eyes in Clover's mane before giving Mom and Harry a hug. "Bye!"

Sophia approached the girls. She particularly liked the look of a girl with a sprig of blue forget-me-nots in her dark, chin-length bob, and she gave her a shy smile. The girl grinned back. Sophia was about to ask her name when a tall lady came toward them. She had a thin, pale face and a long nose with tiny glasses balanced on the end. A girl with wavy brown hair walked confidently by her side. She had sharp green eyes and a long, thin nose just like the teacher's. Sophia smiled at her, but the girl just glared, her nose twitching as if she had smelled something bad.

"Girls," said the teacher abruptly. "I'm Ms. Nettles, your geography and culture teacher. Follow me. You're the last to arrive, and Ms. Primrose is waiting in the hall to pair you with your unicorns. Hurry up. No dawdling."

Sophia fell into step with the dark-haired girl. "Hi, I'm Sophia," she whispered.

"I'm Ava," the girl replied. She nodded at Ms. Nettles. "She looks a bit scary, doesn't she?"

Ms. Nettles's head whipped around. Her skinny neck and mean eyes made her look like a bad-tempered tortoise. "No talking!" she snapped.

Ava made a face at Sophia, who smothered a giggle. A spark of happiness fizzed inside her. She had a feeling that she and Ava were definitely going to be friends!

CHAPTER 2

The girls climbed the marble stairs and went through the huge front door. The school was light and airy with many windows. It was decorated with statues and paintings of unicorns. Ms. Nettles walked so fast that Sophia barely had time to take it all in. It was all very grand, colorful and enormous. Sophia was certain that she'd spend the first week getting lost.

Ms. Nettles finally stopped outside an arched, multicolored glass door that reminded Sophia of Sparkle Lake.

"We are about to enter the hall. You must be

on your best behavior, and please ensure you look neat and tidy before you go in and meet Ms. Primrose."

Sophia pushed her long, wavy hair back over her shoulders. When the new girls had finished fixing their clothes, Ms. Nettles inspected them.

"Lovely, Valentina." She smiled at the brown-haired girl. "Tuck your necklace in, though, dear. Jewelery shouldn't be on show."

"Thanks, Aunt . . . Oops, I mean Ms. Nettles!" Valentina smirked.

"Aunt!" mouthed Ava, widening her eyes.

Sophia widened hers back. "Really!"

"No talking!" snapped Ms. Nettles again.

She led the girls into the hall. Sophia caught her breath. High up, a domed glass roof filled with colored swirls flooded the room with soft rainbow light. Its long rays lit up the magical map positioned in the center of the room. The map

was a model of Unicorn Island in miniature, with snowy mountains, lush green valleys, dusty plains, deep green forests, and sandy beaches. The school, with its lake and fountain, was right in the center of the island. The map was protected by a glimmering magical force field. Sophia's mom had told her that the map was very powerful, and you could visit anywhere on the island just by touching the place you wanted to go to. Sophia longed to try it out, but Mom had said that it was only to be used by teachers and by students who had graduated.

Ms. Nettles marched across the room to where a large group of students were whispering in front of an enormous stage. A regal-looking lady sitting on a high-backed chair watched as Sophia and the others approached. *That must be Ms. Primrose,* thought Sophia. According to Sophia's mom, Ms. Primrose was almost as old as the island itself.

Sophia didn't believe that, but looking at her wrinkled face and pure-white hair, she guessed that Ms. Primrose was very old indeed.

Hearing a whinny, Sophia realized that Ms. Primrose wasn't alone. Waiting in the wings at the side of the stage were young unicorns, all with glimmering snow-white coats, glittering horns, and silky manes and tails. Some of them were hanging back shyly, while others were pushing their way forward, ears pricked.

Ms. Primrose rose to her feet gracefully.

"Good afternoon, everyone." Her voice was low and serious, but Sophia caught a twinkle in her blue eyes. "Welcome to Unicorn Academy. Now that you are ten years old, it is time for you to spend a year here, training and bonding with your own special unicorn. You and your unicorn will be partners for life, helping each other and looking after Unicorn Island."

She paused and gestured toward one of the large windows overlooking the gardens. "Unicorn Academy is a very special place because it is also the home of Sparkle Lake. The lake's waters originate from the center of the earth and flow up through the fountain into the lake and then around the island in rivers and streams. This magical water helps all the people, plants, and animals on Unicorn Island flourish."

She paused and let her gaze fall on every single

student in the room. "During your year at the school, your unicorn should come into his or her magical powers. Some of you are likely to discover this early in the school year, while others will take longer. You will be paired with your unicorn in a moment."

Sophia felt like she was going to burst with excitement. Which unicorn was going to be hers? A few of the young unicorns were pressing forward eagerly, peering out at the students.

There was a beautiful unicorn with long eyelashes and a pale-blue-and-silver tail that swept all the way to the floor; a cheeky-looking unicorn with red-and-gold swirls on her body that matched her mane and tail; and a unicorn with rainbow swirls on his white coat and a rainbow mane and tail. As his lively brown eyes met hers, Sophia's heart flipped. *I want him!* The thought leaped into her head. The unicorn gazed

back at her, and Sophia wondered if he was feeling the same.

Immediately, Sophia felt a flicker of disloyalty as she remembered the promise she'd made to

Clover the night before, when she'd given him his good-night hug. "I'll never love any unicorn as much as I love you," she'd said.

She looked away from the gorgeous rainbow-colored unicorn and focused on what Ms. Primrose was saying.

"When you bond with your unicorn, a lock of your hair will turn the same color as your unicorn's mane. In December, on the longest night of the year, students and their unicorns will graduate at the magnificent Sparkle Lake Ball!"

A ripple of excitement ran through the students. Ms. Primrose turned to the wings. "Sage, please bring the young unicorns out."

A tall, regal unicorn with a stunning gold coat stepped from the side of the stage. His sparkling tail swept along the ground. Sophia gasped. This was the legendary Sage, a wise old unicorn,

distantly descended from the unicorn that had first made the island its home.

Sage led the smaller unicorns out. They followed him down a ramp. They were different heights and colors and they were all gorgeous, but Sophia's eyes kept coming back to the unicorn with the rainbow mane and tail.

Ms. Primrose called out the name of the first student and unicorn. "Valentina de Silva and . . . Golden Briar."

A haughty unicorn with a gold mane trotted daintily to Valentina's side, then stopped and breathed into her outstretched hands. Valentina gave the watching students a superior look. "Thank you, Ms. Primrose," she said grandly. "My parents said you'd give me the best unicorn."

Ms. Primrose looked at Valentina with wise blue eyes. "You have the best unicorn for you, my dear—just like everyone else will."

Valentina look confused as she led Golden Briar away.

I wonder how Ms. Primrose can tell which unicorn we should have, thought Sophia.

Ms. Primrose continued to read out names.

"Ava and . . . Star."

A unicorn with a pale-lilac star on her forehead trotted over to Ava and gently nudged her hand. Ava sent Sophia a delighted smile.

"Sophia . . ."

Hearing Ms. Primrose say her name, Sophia held her breath, her eyes scanning the remaining unicorns. Which one was she going to have? Would it be the unicorn with the rainbow mane and tail she felt so drawn to, or maybe the cute unicorn with a swirling pattern of blue over his coat, or the cheeky unicorn with the red-and-gold mane? Sophia's heart somersaulted. Which one was it going to be?

CHAPTER 3

"Sophia and . . . Rainbow," announced Ms. Primrose.

The unicorn with the rainbow mane whinnied in delight. Sophia's heart leaped as he trotted over and stopped in front of her. She held out her hands. "Rainbow," she whispered.

He nuzzled her hands. "Hello, Sophia. As soon as I saw you, I knew I wanted you to be my friend."

"I felt the same." She felt a thrill of excitement as his lips tickled her fingers. Her very own unicorn! Oh, they were going to have so much

fun together. *But not as much fun as I have with Clover,* she thought quickly, pulling her hands back.

Rainbow sent her a puzzled look as if he sensed her confusion.

Ms. Primrose continued pairing students and unicorns until only a floppy-haired blond boy with a big smile and a unicorn with an electric-blue mane and tail were left. "Billy and Lightning," she said.

As Billy and Lightning completed the circle, everyone started to chatter. "Quiet, please," said Ms. Primrose, clapping her hands. "You can now spend the afternoon exploring the grounds. You may go riding with your unicorns if you wish."

Sophia's excitement grew. She loved riding Clover, but he was so slow these days. Rainbow looked full of energy, impatiently dancing on his hooves as he waited for Ms. Primrose to finish.

"After you've finished exploring, please take your unicorns back to the stable before you clean yourselves up for dinner. You will find your suitcase in your room. There are six dorms with either six girls or six boys in each."

Ms. Primrose told everyone whom they were sharing with. Sophia was in the Sapphire dorm with Ava. How lucky!

At last, Ms. Primrose smiled and said,

"Have fun exploring the grounds. Your lessons start tomorrow."

Sophia grinned at Ava. As she led Rainbow out of the hall, she glanced at the other girls in Sapphire. There was serious-looking Layla, with dark hair long enough to sit on; smiley Scarlett, her blond hair pulled back with a diamond hair clip; Isabel, with brown curls held back with a headband; and redheaded Olivia, with mischievous green eyes. Would they all be friends? Sophia hoped so.

Layla went toward a side door, saying, "Dancer wants me to see his stable first."

Olivia and her unicorn, Snowflake, followed her. Scarlett and Isabel went off with their unicorns, Blaze and Cloud, daring each other to a race, leaving Ava and Sophia together.

"Star is going to show me the lake," said Ava, who had already jumped onto Star's back.

"Do you want to come with us?"

"Yes, please." Sophia couldn't wait to dip her hands in the rainbow-colored water. She'd known about its importance since she was little. Sophia almost had to pinch herself to believe that she was now at school right next to it.

"Aren't you going to get on?" asked Rainbow, nudging Sophia toward his back.

Sophia desperately wanted to ride Rainbow but was hesitating because it made her feel disloyal to Clover. But she could hardly say no, could she? She grinned and jumped onto Rainbow's back. Before she even had a chance to sit properly, he whinnied in delight and took off.

"Whoa!" Sophia grabbed a handful of colored mane.

"Off we go!" shouted Rainbow.

Pulling herself up straight on his back, Sophia began to feel excitement swooping through her as

Rainbow galloped around the gardens. "Faster!" she gasped as her dark hair blew out behind her. All thoughts disappeared from her head apart from the feeling of speed and Rainbow's warm back beneath her. This was like flying!

Rainbow raced across the grass toward the lake. Sophia caught her breath. Glittering in the January sunlight, the multicolored water was even

more beautiful close up. Rainbow didn't stop but plunged straight in, sending a spray of colored droplets raining over Sophia.

She squealed as the cold water hit her and then, laughing, leaned down and hugged his neck. "That was amazing!"

"It was! This is the happiest day of my life," declared Rainbow, reaching around and nuzzling

her leg. "We're going to have lots of adventures and be best friends forever!"

A picture of Clover suddenly popped into Sophia's mind. Poor Clover. How could she have forgotten about him so quickly? She hoped her mom and Harry would remember to rub ointment into his legs when they got home and that he liked molasses in his bran mash at suppertime. She stroked Rainbow's neck, wishing Clover could be at the school too.

"We will be best friends, won't we?" Rainbow said hopefully.

Sophia wanted to say yes, but how could she when Clover was her best friend? She was saved from replying by Ava trotting up to the lake on Star. "You two are wild!" she said, grinning at Sophia and Rainbow. "Star and I had no chance of keeping up with you."

Star dipped her muzzle into the lake and flicked

water up at Rainbow. "Show off!" she teased. "You didn't have to go so fast."

Rainbow snorted. "Why not? I like galloping, and so does Sophia. I've got the best unicorn rider ever!"

"No, I do," said Star.

"I do!" said Rainbow.

The two unicorns bickered affectionately as Rainbow waded out of the lake to join Star.

"The lake is beautiful," said Ava.

Star nodded. "It is, but something seems different today." She put her nose to the water again and sniffed it delicately.

"What do you mean?" Rainbow plunged his whole head into the water and then shook droplets everywhere, making Sophia giggle. "It seems the same to me."

Star looked puzzled. "Don't you think it smells a bit different, and the colors look a little dull?"

"Possibly," Rainbow said slowly. "But if there's a problem, Ms. Primrose will definitely know about it. Sage said she knows everything!" He snorted. "Come on, we're supposed to be exploring! Where shall we go next?"

"I don't care," said Sophia. "But I want to see everything!"

Rainbow whinnied eagerly, and the four friends set off side by side.

CHAPTER 4

The stables were amazing! Everything was so clean and shiny. Sophia loved the silver water troughs that filled up magically with the brightly colored lake water, and she was impressed with the remote-controlled carts that moved bales of straw and piles of sky berries around. There were six rows of stables, each with a storeroom that doubled as a feed room. Outside were two sand rings, and there was an enclosed one that was covered with a dome of hexagonal glass panes, with jumps laid out inside. Sophia looked at them in excitement. She couldn't wait to jump with Rainbow.

Rainbow sensed her excitement. "We'll jump really high together, won't we?"

"We will," Sophia promised him.

Rainbow whinnied happily.

After looking around the stables, Sophia and Ava rode Rainbow and Star back out to the school grounds. Rainbow suggested they gallop again, but Sophia made an excuse. Galloping had been amazing, but she didn't like that it had made her forget about Clover so easily.

The school was surrounded by gardens, where an army of gardeners was hard at work. Where the gardens ended, there was a maze and a play area, with jumps for the unicorns and a merry-go-round and swings for the students. Beyond that were woods, and in the other direction was a cross-country course, with notices saying that both areas were out of bounds unless students were accompanied by a teacher. Someone was

riding a unicorn with an electric-blue mane and tail over the cross-country jumps. Sophia recognized the unicorn and his blond-haired rider. "Billy and Lightning!" she called.

Billy didn't look embarrassed at being caught breaking a rule, and he waved cheerfully.

"Race you back to the stables, girls!" Billy yelled, wheeling Lightning around.

"We're not racing!" shouted Ava.

"I am!" shouted Rainbow.

"Wait!" cried Sophia.

But Rainbow wasn't listening. Head stretched forward, he galloped after Lightning. Wind rushed at Sophia's face and her hair streamed behind her as Rainbow flew along. He was galloping so fast that his hooves barely touched the ground. It felt amazing, and she gave in to the rush of excitement that was surging through her, leaning forward and urging him on.

Rainbow caught up to Lightning, and they raced side by side.

"We're gonna beat you!" whooped Billy.

"Come on, Rainbow!" Sophia cried as the stables came into sight.

Rainbow leaped forward and reached the gate first.

"We won!" Sophia's brown eyes shone as Billy and Lightning pulled up alongside.

"This time," said Billy amicably. "But you wait. We'll get you back."

"Never!" declared Rainbow, stamping his hoof, his dark eyes sparkling.

Dinner was in the dining hall, a long room with glass windows overlooking the lake. At night, it was lit by hundreds of tiny white lights, and it sparkled prettily in the dark. Sophia was hungry after such a busy afternoon, and she piled food onto her plate from the dishes set out on a long counter. Dinner was delicious cheese-topped lasagna, freshly baked garlic bread, and salad. The drinks fountain was a miniature copy of the one in the lake and dispensed water and twenty types of fruit juice.

"It's been a wonderful day," said Ava as she and Sophia walked to their dorm after dinner.

"Wonderful," agreed Sophia.

Sapphire dorm had a sparkly blue door with matching curtains. There were six beds, three

35

on each side, all covered with blue-and-silver blankets. Each girl had a small wardrobe and dresser to put her things in. Lamps lit by shiny sapphire stones softly illuminated the room.

Sophia set out her things: a lucky horseshoe—Clover's, of course—and a photo of Mom, Harry, and Clover. Despite her amazing day, her stomach twisted suddenly with homesickness as she picked up the photo. She missed her mom and brother, but most of all she missed Clover. She looked at Clover's cute face, his sweet eyes and diamond-shaped blaze. Was he missing her too? *Oh, Clover,* Sophia thought. *I wish I knew that you were okay.* She brushed a small tear away quickly.

"Is this your first time away from home?" Ava appeared at Sophia's side, her face full of concern.

Sophia nodded, not trusting herself to speak in case she burst into tears. She didn't want anyone to think she was a crybaby. She just really missed Clover.

"The first night is always the worst. You'll feel better tomorrow. We're going to be far too busy to be homesick once lessons start."

"Thanks," mumbled Sophia. It was kind of Ava to comfort her, but she didn't think she would feel better in the morning, not without knowing how Clover was doing.

Ava looked at the photo in Sophia's hands. "Is that your pony? He's really sweet. I guess you must be missing him lots."

Sophia nodded. Ava glanced at her face and

then gave her a quick hug. "You'll see him again soon," she said softly. "It will be spring break before you know it."

Sophia hugged Ava back. "Thanks," she said.

Ava smiled understandingly, and they got into their pajamas.

The small beds were very comfortable. The moment Sophia snuggled under her feather-filled blanket her eyes started to droop. She was surprised when, next thing she knew, the room was lit with bright sunlight.

"It's so cold," she muttered, shivering as she pulled on a thick hoodie. Sophia came from the west, where even in the rainy season the weather was warm.

Ava rolled out of bed and landed in a heap on the floor. "Ouch," she groaned. "This bed is smaller than mine at home."

After breakfast, all the new first years were split

into two groups. Everyone from Sapphire dorm was in a group with the boys from Diamond dorm and the girls from Emerald. With both cheeky Billy and stuck-up Valentina in her class, Sophia knew things would be interesting. She was pleased that the first lesson was in the stables with Ms. Rosemary, who was both her new advisor and the Care of Unicorns teacher. Valentina led the way there, bragging loudly about the fantastic Golden Briar to two girls from her dorm.

"Golden Briar and I are practically bonded already. I expect he will be the first unicorn to discover his magic. I can't wait to tell my parents! They're both school directors, you know."

Ava raised her eyebrows, and Sophia giggled.

Ms. Rosemary was waiting for the class in the stables with her own unicorn, who had a pink-and-purple-striped mane.

"Our first lesson is about unicorn care,"

Ms. Rosemary told the assembled students. "Who can tell me what unicorns like to eat?"

Valentina yawned loudly. "Easy peasy, lemon squeezy," she whispered in a bored voice.

Ms. Rosemary frowned at her. "Wrong, Valentina. Unicorns don't eat lemons or peas."

There was a shout of laughter. Valentina looked like she might stamp her foot. She scowled, silencing the giggles of her two new friends.

A girl from Sophia's dorm put up her hand. "Yes, Layla?" said Ms. Rosemary.

"A unicorn's favorite food is sky berries, collected from the mountains behind the school," Layla said shyly. "They also need to drink the lake water every day, as this strengthens their magic."

"Very good," said Ms. Rosemary. "If unicorns do not drink the lake water, their powers will start to fade and they may become ill."

The teacher looked around at the group. "Don't forget, your unicorns love your company. They also love being groomed and getting lots of attention, and this will help you to bond. So our first lesson is going to be learning how to braid your unicorn's mane and tail. Follow me, girls and boys!"

CHAPTER 5

Clutching a length of sparkly silver ribbons in one hand and a grooming box in the other, Sophia joined Rainbow in his stall. The unicorn whickered in delight.

"Are the ribbons for me? Are you going to braid them into my mane and tail?"

"I am," said Sophia, stroking Rainbow's neck. "But first I'm going to groom you. You've got sky-berry juice on your face."

Sophia hung the ribbons in Rainbow's stall. But before she could reach for a brush, a scream rang out.

"Aaargh! Help! There's a gross frog with bulgy eyes in my grooming kit."

Valentina! Sophia recognized her shrill voice at once.

"And there's one in mine!"

"Mine too! Ugh! Yuck!"

Sophia went to the door of Rainbow's stall. There was chaos in the stables. Valentina had clambered into a hay trough for safety, where she was fending off three other girls who were trying to climb up too. The floor was covered with frogs, with lumpy blue skin and huge orange eyes.

43

"Don't hurt them! Everyone, stand still," said Ava, rushing past Sophia with a bucket half-filled with water. Kneeling down, she began carefully putting the frogs into it.

Sophia went to help. There was a large frog in her own grooming kit, and she scooped it up in her hands and then went in search of a bucket too. When the last frog had been rescued, the boys sauntered in, led by Billy. Sophia guessed at once from his amused expression that he'd been behind the prank.

"Boys!" said Ava angrily, and strode toward Billy. She didn't even reach his shoulder, but she put her hands on her hips and glared at him. "That was really mean of you. The poor frogs! You shouldn't treat animals that way."

Sophia blinked in surprise. Ava was so gentle and sweet, but she clearly had a temper too.

"I hate it when people are unkind to animals!"

Ava continued. "I won't let it happen!"

Billy lifted his hands. "Whoa! Okay, we're sorry. We won't do it again."

"You'd better not!" said Ava, fixing him with a glare that was worthy of Ms. Nettles. "Where did you find these frogs?"

"In a pond in the woods—" Billy broke off as Ms. Rosemary came up behind them.

"What's going on here?" asked the teacher.

The boys shuffled their feet uneasily.

"Nothing, Ms. Rosemary," said Ava, holding the bucket behind her back.

Sophia was glad Ava hadn't told Ms. Rosemary that the boys had been responsible. As annoying as the prank had been, the frogs hadn't been hurt. Sophia had a feeling that the boys would think twice about playing a trick like that again—especially when Ava was around!

At lunchtime, instead of going to the dining hall, Sophia, Rainbow, Ava, and Star sneaked away to the woods. Sophia and Ava each carried a bucket of frogs.

"Are you sure this is a good idea?" asked Ava. "The woods are out of bounds, and I've heard they're really dangerous."

"We won't need to go far," said Sophia. "Billy said they'd only just started exploring the woods on a dare when they found the frogs."

"Be careful, everyone," said Star. "There are dangerous creatures in here."

Rainbow snorted. "I wonder if we'll meet any!"

The four of them entered the woods. The thick canopy of leaves overhead blocked out the sunlight and the air felt cold as they rode down a path that twisted its way around thorny bushes and ancient tree trunks.

Sophia shivered and wrapped her hands in

46

Rainbow's thick mane to keep them warm. The woods did feel scary and dangerous. She glanced at the shadows, wondering what might be hiding there.

Rainbow pushed through some brambles as the path narrowed. Sophia looked into the bucket to check that the frogs were okay and frowned. "Weird. The water in this bucket has changed! It was dusty and dirty before, but now it's totally clear. Has yours changed too?" she asked Ava.

Ava checked. "Yes!" she said in surprise.

"It must be something to do with the frogs," said Star.

Ava looked thoughtful. "It could be. Maybe there's some magic in them."

"Look! Is that the pond?" exclaimed Rainbow. He trotted down the path toward a grove of small trees and pushed his way through the branches. "Yes! We're here!" he said as he stepped into a

clearing. The pond water was glittering just like the water in the buckets. There were lots of frogs perched on lily pads or diving into the water, and butterflies fluttered through the sunlit air.

The frogs in the bucket started croaking excitedly.

"I think we've come to the right place," Ava said with a grin.

She and Sophia dismounted and carefully carried the frogs over to the pond. They kneeled down, and the frogs leaped happily into the water.

"Home at last," said Sophia, emptying the water out of the bucket.

"Now *we'd* better get back home," said Star, looking around anxiously. "I don't like these woods. They feel creepy."

They remounted, and the unicorns cantered back down the path. As they burst out of the trees into the warm rays of the sun and saw the lake sparkling in front of them, Sophia felt a rush of relief. "Race you back!" she cried. Rainbow and Star whinnied and galloped across the short grass toward the stables.

The first couple of weeks whizzed by. Sophia's favorite lessons were the ones taught outside with the unicorns. Often, her class would ride around the grounds, learning about different environments and how best to care for them. Ava loved outdoor lessons just as much as Sophia did. She persuaded the head gardener to give her a patch of the kitchen garden. Ava was proud of the herbs and edible plants she started to grow, and spent hours tending them. Sophia helped her, and in return Ava went riding with Sophia, jumping fallen trees and having races.

The days were so busy that Sophia didn't have much time to think about Clover. But at night, lying in bed, Sophia couldn't stop worrying about her old pony and feeling guilty at how well she was getting along with Rainbow. The unicorn was such fun, and Sophia loved his lively nature.

One afternoon at the end of the second week, Sophia and Ava were out riding, looking for some rare blue winter poppies so Ava could collect some seeds, when they came across Lucy, a girl from Ruby dorm, sitting on the path. Her unicorn, Cherry, was peering down at Lucy's ankle.

"Are you all right?" Sophia asked.

Lucy grimaced. "Not really. I tripped and now I can't stand up."

As Sophia and Ava dismounted to try to help, Cherry nuzzled Lucy's ankle, blowing softly on it. Pink sparkles flew out of her nostrils, and the air smelled like burnt sugar.

"Oooh, that feels nice," said Lucy as the sparkles swirled around her ankle. "It's taking the pain away."

Cherry's eyes widened. "I don't know where those sparkles came from."

"It must be magic!" said Ava.

Cherry continued to blow sparkles onto Lucy's foot until she was able to scramble up again.

"That's amazing, Cherry!" she cried.

"You've got healing powers," gasped Sophia, staring at Cherry in awe.

"Yes, I do," said Cherry, snorting with

excitement. "I can feel magic tingling inside me. Hooray!"

Magic sparkles hung in the air as Cherry and Lucy hugged. Sophia felt a pang of envy, but she smiled brightly.

"That'll be you soon," she whispered to Rainbow. "I wonder what your powers will be! You'll discover your magic before long. I just know you will!"

CHAPTER 6

Cherry was the first unicorn to discover her magical power. The news spread through the school like wildfire and everyone buzzed with excitement. Apart from Valentina, of course, who just scowled and said it had been a fluke. Sophia ignored her and wondered who would be next.

One morning, after a grooming lesson, Ms. Rosemary asked her class to line up with their unicorns for an inspection. Rainbow's coat shone in the winter sunlight, and he arched his neck, proudly showing off the ribbons that Sophia had braided through his mane.

When Sophia and Rainbow joined Valentina at the start of the line, Rainbow tickled Golden Briar with his tail. "Look at me," he said proudly. "Don't I look good?"

Golden Briar whipped around and nipped Rainbow sharply on the neck. "Keep your horrible tail away from me!"

"Ouch, that hurt!" cried Rainbow, shocked.

Tossing his head, Golden Briar turned his back on Rainbow, aiming a kick at him for good measure.

Valentina put her nose in the air. "It's your own fault, Rainbow. You shouldn't stand next to a unicorn like Golden Briar. You don't have any gold on you anywhere, and everyone knows the best unicorns have to have gold. You should go to the end of the line where you belong." Her two friends giggled. Valentina smirked at them. "In fact, if you don't move away from me and Golden Briar right now, I shall speak to my parents. They're trustees here, and they'll make sure that you know your place."

"Excuse me!" Sophia was so angry that she spluttered out her words. "How dare you speak to Rainbow like that! He's brilliant!"

Valentina laughed meanly. "Brilliant at being stupid."

Sophia lost her temper. "You're the stupid one, Valentina!" she snapped. "You think you're so great and so important, but hardly anyone likes

56

you! Maybe *you* should go to the end of the line!"

There were a few whoops and cheers from the rest of the group.

"You tell her, Sophia!" called Billy.

Valentina's eyes narrowed. "Why, you . . . !"

"Whatever is all the commotion about?" said Ms. Rosemary, hurrying over with her unicorn, Blossom.

"It was all Sophia's fault," said Valentina quickly. "She's being really mean to me!" Her voice rose into a fake wail, and her two friends quickly put their arms around her.

Ms. Rosemary frowned. "Sophia?" she said questioningly.

Sophia hesitated. She didn't like tattling.

"It wasn't Sophia's fault," Ava said, stepping forward. "Valentina started it. She insulted Rainbow." There were murmurs of agreement from some of the other girls.

57

"Hmmm." Ms. Rosemary looked from Sophia to the loudly sobbing Valentina. "Well, I think we should all just get on with the lesson. Valentina, the ribbons are coming loose in Golden Briar's mane. Stop crying now and go sort them out. Rainbow looks lovely, Sophia, but would you like some of my silver polish for his hooves as a finishing touch?"

"Yes, please," said Sophia, glad not to be in trouble.

Ms. Rosemary turned to her unicorn. "Please, could you magic it here for me, Blossom?"

"Of course," said Blossom. Her powers let her transport objects from one place to another by magic. "The silver hoof polish from the storeroom!" she declared, tossing her long pink-and-purple mane.

A few sparkles floated up into the air, but then they winked and went out. No hoof polish appeared. Blossom looked confused.

"The silver hoof polish from the storeroom!" she repeated with another mane toss. But this time there were no sparkles and the hoof polish still didn't appear.

Blossom looked at Ms. Rosemary. "My magic's not working."

Ms. Rosemary frowned. "How odd. Last week, Ms. Lavender's unicorn was struggling with his healing magic. This is very strange."

"Is something wrong with the unicorns?" Layla asked anxiously.

"Don't worry. I'm sure everything's fine,"

said Ms. Rosemary. She patted Blossom. "You're probably just tired, or coming down with a bug or something."

"But what about Ms. Lavender's unicorn?" said Scarlett.

"Maybe all the unicorns are coming down with a bug!" said Olivia in alarm.

"That's enough, girls," said Ms. Rosemary firmly. "I'm sure there's a very simple explanation for this. Back to grooming, everyone. Five minutes and then it's final inspection time. Sophia, why don't you take Rainbow to the storeroom and paint his hooves there?"

Sophia nodded and walked off with Rainbow. She felt worried about the teachers' unicorns, and she was still angry with Valentina. Rainbow nuzzled Sophia's shoulder. "Thank you for sticking up for me before."

"Valentina and Golden Briar are horrible," said Sophia. "You don't need gold anywhere. You're perfect just the way you are."

Rainbow nuzzled her hands. "I think you're the best, Sophia."

Sophia wanted to say she thought he was too, but the words were stuck in her throat. She loved Clover. It felt so disloyal.

Rainbow was looking at her expectantly. She gave him a quick hug. "You're such a special unicorn," she said quickly. "The best unicorn ever."

Sophia saw Rainbow's hurt look, and she felt dreadful. She cleared her throat. "Now, I wonder where this silver polish is. You wait out here and I'll go and get it."

She hurried into the storeroom and away from the hurt look in her unicorn's eyes.

CHAPTER 7

After that day's lesson, Valentina really had it in for Sophia. She made lots of nasty remarks when the teachers weren't around and giggled and whispered with her two friends, pointing at Sophia when they were in the dining hall or riding. Sophia ignored her. She didn't have time for Valentina's silly games. There was so much to do and learn, and there was the thing that the whole school was talking about—what was affecting the unicorns' powers?

"Did you hear what happened in the gardens?" Ava said to Sophia after they'd been to the stables

62

to see Star. "One of the unicorns in second year was trying to help the gardeners by making it rain in the vegetable patch, but she lost control of her rain powers and caused an enormous flood!"

"That's awful!" said Sophia.

"I know," said Ava, shaking her head gloomily.

Later that day, Ms. Primrose put up a notice to say that the playground was out of bounds.

"One of the students was working with his unicorn to make a daisy grow when she accidentally caused an earthquake," Sophia told Ava, having heard it from Rainbow. "Apparently the earth just exploded!"

"What's going on?" said Ava. "Star says the unicorns' magic has never gone wrong like this before." She went to the dorm window. "Do you think there's something wrong with the lake? It isn't looking as bright as usual, and, remember, Star said it smelled a bit strange."

Sophia joined her at the window and looked out across the lake. "You're right, it isn't glittering much," she said. "And it looks a bit yellow." Sophia turned to Ava anxiously. "What if something bad is going on? Maybe someone is trying to harm the unicorns."

Ava shook her head. "That can't be right. No one would do that."

However, the next day in assembly, Ms. Primrose made a dreadful announcement.

"I am very sorry to have to break this news, but it's come to my attention that someone has been tampering with the lake."

A hum of chatter rose.

"Do you think it's the boys playing a prank?" Ava whispered to Sophia.

"No, the boys are annoying, but they wouldn't harm the unicorns," Sophia said.

"Quiet, please!" said Ms. Primrose sharply.

"The person responsible for this should know that their actions are irresponsible and very dangerous. By contaminating the water, this person is putting our unicorns' well-being at risk. I really hope no student is responsible. If it *is* a student, and they are caught, they will be expelled from the school. If the situation continues, then the school will be forced to close. Students and unicorns will be separated and sent home for their own safety."

There was a collective gasp.

Ava looked at Sophia. "What are we going to do? I don't want to go home, and I'm definitely not leaving without Star."

Sophia hesitated. She couldn't help thinking that if they got sent home, she could see her family and Clover again.

But it would mean leaving Rainbow, she reminded herself. She felt torn in half. Part of

65

her desperately wanted to be with Clover, but she couldn't imagine life without Rainbow now.

"Quiet, please," called Ms. Primrose. "I hope we can resolve this issue before we have to take such drastic action. If anyone has any information about what's happening, I hope you will come and tell me. Off you go to your lessons."

As the students turned to leave, Sophia saw Valentina whispering to the boy next to her and then nodding in Sophia's direction. The boy seemed surprised, and he stared at Sophia. He then whispered something to the boy standing beside him.

Sophia sighed. "What's Valentina saying about me now?"

"Just ignore it," murmured Ava. "You know what she's like."

Sophia turned away, determined not to let Valentina's nastiness upset her.

But it wasn't that easy. Valentina was clearly spreading mean gossip about her. Sophia could tell from the way people stopped talking whenever she approached them. Things came to a head at the start of a lesson on the magical properties of unicorns. Sophia was setting out her pens when Scarlett and Isabel stopped in front of her desk.

"Is it true?" demanded Scarlett. "Have you been messing with the lake?"

"Excuse me?" Sophia wasn't sure she'd heard right.

"Did you put something in the lake?" asked Isabel. "Valentina's been telling everyone you have. She said you did it as a joke."

"And that you were smiling when Ms. Primrose was talking about it in assembly," added Isabel. "One of the boys saw you smiling too."

Sophia felt as if she'd just had a bucket of ice dumped over her. "I wouldn't do that! I would never harm any of the unicorns or hurt the lake's magic. I was smiling because I was thinking about my pony at home."

Scarlett and Isabel exchanged glances.

"We believe you," said Scarlett. "We didn't really think you would be so mean, but we needed to check. Valentina's also been saying she saw you by the lake the other night."

"Well, she's lying!" said Sophia furiously.

"Girls, go to your seats, please."

Scarlett and Isabel scuttled away as Ms. Rosemary bustled into the room. Sophia fiddled with her pens angrily. How could Valentina spread such a terrible lie? At least Scarlett and Isabel had believed her when she'd denied it, but as dorm friends, they knew her better than most people did. What about the rest of the school? What if they believed Valentina?

The day passed in an unhappy blur for Sophia. Wherever she went in the school, she was certain people were whispering about her. When she got to the stables with Ava after lunch, Rainbow sensed her unhappiness, but Sophia refused to tell him why she was upset.

"It's nothing. I'm just not feeling like myself," she lied, not wanting to talk about it in case it upset him.

"Why didn't you tell Rainbow the truth?" said

69

Ava as they went back to the dorm later on. "He's your friend."

"I can't!" Sophia turned her back on Ava as she felt tears fill her eyes. "If I did, Rainbow would probably start an argument with Golden Briar. I don't want him to get into trouble over me."

"You still should have told him," Ava said, her brown eyes serious. "It's wrong to keep secrets from your unicorn."

Sophia had a restless night, waking regularly, her stomach in knots at how unfair Valentina was being. She hated people at school thinking she'd do anything to damage the island, and she knew Ava was right. She shouldn't have lied to Rainbow.

At dawn, she silently got up and dressed. She was close to tears and wanted to talk to Rainbow. As she reached the door, she saw that a folded piece of paper had been pushed under it with her name written on it. Curiously, she opened it.

> WE KNOW YOU DID IT!
> OWN UP OR WE'LL TELL
> MS. PRIMROSE!
> PEOPLE LIKE YOU
> SHOULDN'T BE AT
> THIS SCHOOL.

Sophia's heart hammered against her rib cage as she reread the note. Who had sent it? Was it Valentina or someone else? It made her sick to her stomach. Swallowing a silent sob, she crumpled the paper up, threw it onto the floor, and wrenched open the door. She raced across the dew-soaked lawn to the stables. Rainbow was still asleep. He looked so sweet with his long eyelashes

and eyes shut tight. Sophia couldn't hold back her tears any longer.

"Sophia!" Rainbow said, waking in alarm. "What's the matter?"

Throwing herself down beside him, Sophia flung her arms around his neck and sobbed. "Everyone thinks I'm the one hurting the lake!" she cried. "Oh, Rainbow! I can't bear it—I want to go home!" She told him everything—all about the lies that Valentina was spreading and how much she missed Clover and how worried she was that he was unhappy without her.

Rainbow nuzzled her as she sobbed.

"You're the best unicorn ever, Rainbow," she told him, scrubbing away her tears. "You really are. But I don't want to stay here any longer." She took a deep breath. "I'm going to run away!"

CHAPTER 8

Rainbow snorted in alarm. "No, Sophia! You can't run away! I know you're missing Clover, but you belong here. Just tell the teachers that Valentina is lying."

Sophia hugged herself. "Valentina's parents are trustees. No one will believe me. I have to go."

"You don't!" Rainbow shook his head and jumped to his feet. "I'll help you clear your name."

Sophia shook her head. "No."

Rainbow stamped a hoof. "Stay or I'll tell the teachers and then they'll stop you from leaving!"

Sophia gasped. "You'd really tell the teachers?"

Rainbow nodded. "I'm not going to just let you go. You're my best friend."

"Friends don't break each other's trust!" exclaimed Sophia.

"Friends don't run away from each other!" snapped Rainbow.

Fighting back more tears, Sophia ran from the stables. Just when she'd thought things couldn't get worse, she'd argued with Rainbow! She didn't know what to do. She looked at the clock, high on the outside of the hayloft. There was still enough time to go back to the dorm for her things and leave before anyone woke. It would take ages to get home, but she couldn't bear to stay at school any longer.

Sophia hurried across the grass toward the school building. In the distance, she noticed a tall figure dressed in dark trousers and a cloak walking near the lake. Something about the

stealthy way the person was moving made Sophia duck down behind a bush. Who was that? What were they doing so early in the morning? Reaching the lakeside, the figure stopped and looked around. Sophia peered out over the top of the bush.

With lightning speed, the figure reached into a pocket and scattered something into the lake. The moment it hit the water, the lake bubbled and hissed. The person watched for a moment, then hurried toward a side door in the school. A sour smell rose in the air.

Sophia cried out with worry as the water turned a sickly shade of yellow. She jumped to her feet, anger boiling in her stomach. Who was under the cloak? Why would anyone want to do such a dreadful thing to Sparkle Lake? Everyone knew Unicorn Island depended on its water.

There was only one way to find out what was going on. Sophia followed the figure into the school. The corridor was empty, but a trail of wet footprints led straight to the hall. Sophia peeked inside. Early-morning sunlight streamed through the domed glass ceiling, illuminating the empty room and making the magical map shimmer. Sophia stared around, her eyes coming back to the map. There was no one here. Had the mysterious figure used the map to escape?

Her footsteps echoed as she crossed to the middle of the hall. There were several splotches

of colored lake mud on Sophia's side of the barrier, but it was impossible to tell if the map had been used.

"Sophia!" a voice whispered. "What are you doing?"

Sophia spun around. "Ava! Why are you here?"

"I was looking for you. I saw your bed was empty, and then I found this!" Ava held out the note that Sophia had crumpled up. "How could anyone write such mean things? I thought you'd run away." Ava gave Sophia a hug.

"I was about to," said Sophia truthfully. "But that's not important now. We need to talk!" She pulled Ava along the corridor until she reached a quiet nook. Ava glanced out the window. The lake had turned mustardy yellow.

"Eeew!" Ava's eyes widened. "Why is the lake that color?"

Quickly, Sophia told Ava everything.

Ava was shocked. "You mustn't run away, Sophia. I'd miss you tons. Everyone in our dorm would. Everyone likes you, apart from stupid Valentina, and everyone knows that you wouldn't harm the lake."

Looking into Ava's earnest eyes, Sophia felt her confusion and unhappiness fade slightly.

"Go to Rainbow and tell him you're sorry,"

urged Ava. "He'll be feeling awful that you've argued."

Sophia nodded. "I will," she decided. "But first we need to do something about the lake."

"Should we wake Ms. Rosemary and tell her?" suggested Ava.

"No," said Sophia. "I think we should fix it ourselves. That will prove it wasn't me. We just need a plan."

"Frogs!" said Ava, almost sliding off the window seat with excitement.

"Frogs?"

"The frogs in the woods!" Ava nodded, her dark hair swinging at her chin. "Remember the way the frogs we caught made the dirty water in the buckets sparkle?"

"Yes . . . ," said Sophia.

"Maybe those frogs have the power to purify

water! If we could put some in the lake, then they might be able to make it healthy again."

"Brilliant idea—" Sophia broke off suddenly, putting a finger to her lips to silence Ava.

"What is it?" mouthed Ava.

Sophia looked up and down the corridor. It was empty in both directions. "Nothing," she said, giving a small laugh. "For a second I thought I heard someone."

Ava touched her arm in reassurance. "There's no one here but us, and we need to act fast to save the lake. Let's go to the woods now and get the frogs."

"Good idea," said Sophia. She grabbed Ava's hand, and they ran full speed toward the stables.

CHAPTER 9

The girls charged into the stable. Rainbow's eyes brightened. "Sophia," he whickered. "You haven't run away! What made you change your mind?"

"The lake!" Sophia gasped. "We need to go to the woods."

"We'll explain as we go," said Ava hurriedly as she led Star to the door.

In next to no time, Rainbow and Star were galloping across the grounds toward the woods, the girls each clutching a bucket to carry the frogs in. Rainbow's silky mane blew into Sophia's

face, tickling her nose. Sophia laughed. She was on her way to save the lake and clear her name! "You said we'd have adventures, Rainbow! Well, I think this is our first one!" she cried.

Rainbow neighed in delight.

The gardens passed by in a blur. As they reached the woods, Rainbow slowed. The gloomy woods felt cold, and strange hoots and screeches came from the shadows.

Star's ears flickered nervously. "I'm scared. I feel like something bad is going to happen."

"We'll be fine. We just need to find the frogs and get out of here fast," said Ava.

The unicorns cantered along the path, jumping the tree roots that seemed to want to trip them up.

There was a howl in the trees. Both unicorns skittered nervously. Sophia patted Rainbow's neck.

"I like it when you do that," said Rainbow. "It makes me feel braver."

Sophia stroked Rainbow again, and he whickered with delight.

They reached the grove and pushed their way through the trees. They could hear the frogs croaking as they stepped into the clearing. Sophia blinked in the morning sunlight that streamed from the sky and danced across the surface of the pond. The frogs were everywhere, perched on lily

pads, swimming in the water, or lazily croaking to each other among the weeds. She and Ava dismounted and carefully scooped up the frogs, placing them in the buckets along with some water.

"We'll bring you back as soon as you've worked your magic on the lake," Ava promised.

Sophia had just grabbed a frog from a lily pad when she heard a twig snap behind her.

"Who's there?" She spun around, her eyes searching the tree line.

"I didn't hear anyone," said Rainbow.

Sophia's eyes scanned the woods. They were empty, but she couldn't shake the feeling that someone was

watching. She continued catching frogs, but every now and then she glanced around, just in case.

"That should be enough," said Ava, when each bucket was half full of frogs. She and Sophia jumped back on their unicorns and set off to the school.

The woods seemed darker after the brightness of the clearing. Sophia couldn't wait to be out of them. The rustling bushes were making her nervous. She stared around. What was that? Sophia's heart drummed as she caught sight of a figure moving through the trees.

Goose bumps prickled along Sophia's arms. The figure was dressed in dark clothes with a mask covering their face, just like the person she'd seen earlier tipping something into the lake! "Rainbow," she whispered. "Follow that figure!"

Rainbow changed direction, plunging into the trees with Star following silently behind. The

person hurried along an uphill path. At the top, they momentarily disappeared from view. The unicorns sped up and found themselves on the crest of a grassy hill. The path went down a steep slope into a valley. The mysterious figure had disappeared.

"They must be farther down the hill!" said Rainbow.

"We've got to catch them!" said Sophia. "Come on!"

"We need to be careful," Star called anxiously. "Remember, the woods are dangerous."

But Rainbow and Sophia were already cantering toward a heap of rust-colored leaves at the bottom of the valley. Ava and Star raced after them. As they approached the pile, Sophia frowned. Something wasn't right. What was it? As Rainbow reached the leaves, she suddenly realized.

"Rainbow, stop!" cried Sophia, as Ava and Star came racing up behind them. "How can these be here? There aren't any trees!"

But it was too late. As Rainbow's and Star's hooves touched the leaves, the ground beneath them gave way. Air rushed past as all four friends plummeted into a trap!

CHAPTER 10

They landed with a jolt in a dark pit.

"Are you okay?" Sophia asked Rainbow.

"I think so. Are you?"

"Yes," said Sophia, checking that the frogs weren't hurt. "But where are we?" As her eyes adjusted to the gloom, she could just make out Ava and Star a step away.

"The person we were following must have set this trap for us," said Ava. "If only we could see more."

A green spark flashed above Rainbow's head, then fizzled away.

Sophia stared around her. Where had the spark come from? A second later, a flash of silver lit the air.

"What is happening?" she said.

"I don't know." Rainbow shook his mane, and more colored sparks swirled around him.

"It's you!" said Sophia. "You're making the sparks!"

"Am I?" Rainbow tossed his head, creating more flashes of light. "You're right. It *is* me! I feel all tingly!"

"It's your magic powers!" said Star in delight.

"Can you use the sparks to light everything up so we can see?" asked Sophia eagerly.

"I can try." Rainbow drew a breath and held his eyes tightly shut as he concentrated. There was a crack, and a ray of white light cut through the darkness.

"Rainbow, that's brilliant!" Sophia was

thrilled. She had wanted Rainbow to have healing powers, but being able to create light was amazing. A bright white beam shone from Rainbow, illuminating everything like an enormous floodlight. Sophia saw they were trapped in a pit with steep sides.

"What's that hissing sound?" asked Ava suddenly.

"Snakes!" squeaked Sophia in dismay, spotting several pythons hissing furiously at the far end of the pit.

Their bodies writhed and they began to slither toward the girls and the unicorns.

"Get back," said Rainbow, his voice wobbling. He shone his light at the snakes, and they reacted angrily, tongues flashing, muscular bodies constricting.

Rainbow trembled. "I . . . I don't like snakes."

His light got fainter. Sophia breathed deeply,

taking control of her own fear. She could feel his sides starting to heave with panic.

"Don't worry. I'm here," she said, frantically wondering what they were going to do. She kissed Rainbow and stroked his neck. "I won't let the snakes hurt you."

Suddenly the smell of burnt sugar filled the air, followed by a sharp crack.

Magic!

Sophia recognized the smell from before, when Cherry had found her power. Rainbow's light beam flared, then a rainbow arched from the top of his head to the top of the pit. Sophia reached out and touched it and realized it was solid—a rainbow bridge!

"Rainbow!" squealed Sophia in delight. "That's amazing."

"Go! I don't know how long I can hold it," Rainbow panted, touching his head to the ground and anchoring the end of the rainbow there.

Star galloped onto the rainbow bridge with Ava hanging on to her bucket of frogs. Rainbow followed hot on her heels.

The pythons hissed with rage and tried to follow them, but the moment Rainbow's hooves reached the top of the pit, the rainbow disappeared. The snakes spat with fury as they fell back into the pit.

"Hurray for Rainbow!" cheered Ava. "I'm so

glad you found your powers before we ended up a snakes' breakfast."

"Are you okay, though? Do you need a rest?" asked Sophia.

Rainbow stood up tall. "I feel amazing! Let's get these frogs to the lake now, before it's too late."

They galloped back through the woods and onto the school grounds. As they neared the lake, Sophia saw a figure hurrying toward them, arms waving angrily as it tried to cut them off. For a second, she thought it was the masked figure from before, but then she realized her mistake.

"It's Ms. Nettles," she said. "And she looks furious."

"Stop!" shouted Ms. Nettles, arms spread wide, blocking the path. "You know the woods are out of bounds. What were you doing in there?"

"There isn't time to explain!" said Sophia. "We have to save the lake! Look at it, Ms. Nettles!"

The lake, a sickly yellow, was now covered with an oily film.

"It's stopped moving," said Star.

"But we can fix it!" said Ava. "We just have to get these frogs there as soon as possible."

Magic sparked around Rainbow as he pointed his head at the lake. A rainbow soared above him, arching right over Ms. Nettles.

"Wait!" shouted Ms. Nettles, but Rainbow galloped across the arch of colored light with Star following.

"Sorry, Ms. Nettles, I promise we'll explain later!" Sophia shouted to the astonished teacher.

CHAPTER 11

As Star's hooves touched the ground, the rainbow dissolved, leaving a trail of colored sparks hanging in the air. At the lakeside, Sophia slid from Rainbow's back. With Ava's help, she carefully tipped both buckets of frogs onto the shore.

"Go, frogs, go!"

The frogs hopped and plopped into the water, croaking as they swam away. Sophia crossed her fingers and wished them luck. The water fizzed and hissed, and sparks crackled off the surface.

Several agonizing minutes later, the water was looking less yellow.

"It's working," gasped Ava. "Well done, little frogs."

"Sophia! Ava! How dare you defy me!" Ms. Nettles puffed up. Her long nose was pinched, and her glasses rattled furiously. "When I tell you to stop, you do so immediately." She stabbed a finger at them. "Such behavior will be punished—"

"The lake!" Ms. Primrose called, seeming to appear from nowhere and cantering toward them on Sage. "Look at the lake!"

Sophia stared at the waters shimmering with every color imaginable, and her heart felt like it was bursting with pride. They'd done it. Not only had she cleared her name, but along with Rainbow, Ava, and Star, she'd stopped the lake from dying and the island from being destroyed.

"Yes, well done, girls," Ms. Nettles said tightly.

Ms. Primrose turned to Sophia and Ava. "What I don't understand is where you got the frogs from, and how you knew that this particular type of frog can purify water. They're incredibly rare creatures."

"We found some frogs hopping out of the woods one day," Sophia said, stretching the truth a bit so as not to get Billy and his friends in trouble. "We took them back and found the pond where they live. We carried them in buckets and noticed they cleaned the water inside. I know we shouldn't have gone into the woods, but we wanted the frogs to be safe."

Ms. Primrose smiled. "I think we can overlook breaking the school rules on this one occasion."

Sophia and Ava explained about the figure Sophia had seen tipping something into the lake that morning. Ms. Primrose's face grew grave as she heard the story. "This is very worrying," she

said. "We shall clearly have to be very vigilant from now on." She looked around. A group of girls were running across the lawn. It was the rest of Sapphire dorm. "However, that is a problem for another time," she said with a smile.

"What's going on?" gasped Scarlett as she charged up. "We woke up and saw Sophia and Ava out here."

"Your friends and their unicorns have managed to save the lake," said Ms. Primrose. "Sophia and Ava can explain, but don't be too long, girls, or you'll miss breakfast. I'll make an announcement to the whole school at assembly and make sure everyone knows how amazing you four have been."

When their friends heard what had happened, they hugged and congratulated Sophia and Ava, and made a huge fuss over Rainbow and Star. Surrounded by her friends, warmth and happiness

spread through Sophia, and she was really glad she hadn't run away.

"You're so lucky, having such an adventure!" said Isabel.

"We'll have to sneak into the woods and explore too," Scarlett told her.

Ava grinned. "Just don't let Ms. Nettles catch you!"

Sophia realized she was starving. "You go ahead and save us a seat at breakfast," she told the others. "We'll catch up to you once Rainbow and Star are settled."

Sophia and Ava cantered the unicorns to the stables and filled their feed buckets with sky berries. Rainbow took a long drink from his water trough, which magically kept refilling from the lake until his thirst was quenched.

"Delicious," he said, shaking the last drops of multicolored water from his lips. He turned to

Sophia and breathed gently on her arm. "I've been thinking," he said. "I know you're missing Clover very much, so I won't stop you from leaving the school if that's what you really want to do."

Sophia threw herself at Rainbow, hugging him tightly. "I don't want to leave the school anymore—and I couldn't bear to leave you. I just wish I could stop worrying about Clover. I've had him since I was tiny."

"If only I could help you," said Rainbow, stamping a front hoof. He snorted with surprise as a shimmery purple light suddenly swirled up from the ground. Golden sparkles fizzed around the edges as the purple light formed into a circle and the sparkles danced across the surface. "What's happening?" he said.

Sophia gasped as a picture appeared in the circle of light. "It must be part of your power. That's our field at home! Look, there's the stable

in the corner. And there's Clover!" Her voice rose. "Look how plump he's getting. Doesn't he look happy?"

Clover pulled up a mouthful of lush green grass and chewed slowly, his eyes sparkling with happiness. In the distance, Harry and Mom were walking toward the field with a bucket of feed and a grooming kit.

Sophia felt happiness rush through her. "He looks as if he isn't missing me at all! Now I can enjoy the school without feeling so guilty." Sophia hugged Rainbow again, but as she pulled away, Rainbow whinnied.

"Look at you!"

He put his muzzle into Sophia's hair and lifted a wavy strand. Sophia caught a flash of rainbow-colored hair and laughed. "We've bonded," she breathed, holding the ringlet out and comparing it to Rainbow's mane. They were identical.

Rainbow whickered in delight, and Sophia suddenly knew that she didn't need to choose between her pony and her unicorn. Bonding with Rainbow didn't mean she had to love Clover any less—the love she had inside her just doubled in size. Throwing her arms around Rainbow's neck, she hugged him tightly.

Leaving Rainbow and Star devouring more sky

berries, Sophia and Ava ran out of the stables. They were greeted by Olivia.

"Come with me!" she cried. "Ms. Primrose said our dorm could have a special picnic breakfast down by the lake. Sage made us a sparkly slide to help us get there."

Sophia turned and saw an amazing glittery slide swooping from the stables to the far side of the lake. At the end of it, Scarlett, Layla, and Isabel were taking food out of a massive basket. Sophia's stomach gurgled hungrily.

"Let's go," she said, grabbing hold of Ava's hand.

Laughing together, they jumped onto the slide and whizzed off to join the rest of their friends.

Magical Sparkle Lake is starting to freeze,
and Unicorn Academy might have to close.
Can Scarlett and Blaze find out who's
freezing the lake and save the school?

Read on for a peek at the next
book in the Unicorn Academy series!

CHAPTER 1

"Higher!" said Scarlett.

Isabel, Scarlett's best friend, raised the branch again, balancing it carefully between a bush and the gnarled trunk of an old tree. It was as high as her head now.

"I think that's too big," said Cloud, Isabel's unicorn, giving the jump a doubtful look.

Scarlett pushed her long blond hair back over her shoulders. Her blue eyes sparkled as she patted her own unicorn's neck. Her cheeks were flushed from the icy breeze, and snowflakes whirled around her.

"It's not too big for us, is it, Blaze?"

"Definitely not. I can clear that easily!" Blaze whickered. The cheeky-looking unicorn with fiery red-and-gold swirls on her snow-white coat loved a challenge, just like Scarlett. "Watch this, Cloud!"

Blaze galloped eagerly at the makeshift jump. Scarlett sank her hands deeper into Blaze's silky mane as she took off, the crisp air making her eyes water. Scarlett loved the feeling of flying and then plunging back down to earth. As Blaze landed, a

few orange sparks flickered up from her hooves and Scarlett caught a faint whiff of burnt sugar.

Isabel gasped. "That was incredible. You jumped so high, I almost thought you were going to fly away!"

Scarlett's heart skipped with hope—the huge jump, the sparks, and the sweet smell. Could that mean Blaze was about to discover her magic power? Every unicorn on Unicorn Island was born with a special magical power—it just took a while for that power to be revealed. Some unicorns could fly, others turned invisible, some could create light or fire. Scarlett couldn't wait for Blaze to discover her power, and she really hoped it would be flying.

Scarlett was ten years old and had recently started at Unicorn Academy, where she had been given her own special unicorn, just like all the other girls and boys who had joined at the

same time. They were all in training to become full-fledged guardians of Unicorn Island, the wonderful land in which they lived.

Scarlett knew she would be able to move up at the end of the year only if Blaze had discovered her magical power and bonded with her. She let her hair fall forward, searching for a red-gold lock of hair to match Blaze's mane that would show they had bonded. But there was no flame-colored strand in her long blond hair yet. Disappointed, Scarlett turned her attention back to the jump.

"Put it up even higher," she called, hoping that if it was big enough, Blaze might actually fly!

"I'll put it up in a minute. It's my turn first," said Isabel, turning Cloud to face the jump. Cloud was a pretty unicorn with gentle brown eyes.

"I think it's too big for me, Isabel," said Cloud anxiously.

"No, it's not," said Isabel. "Blaze jumped it easily. Let's try!"

"Wait, Isabel!" whispered Scarlett as she spotted Ms. Nettles, one of the teachers, cantering over on her unicorn, Thyme.

Isabel ignored her. "Don't be boring, Cloud! Come on. Give it a try!"

"Isabel!" insisted Scarlett. "Behind you!" Of all the teachers to catch them jumping, Ms. Nettles was the worst. She was very strict, with a fierce temper.

"Isabel!" Ms. Nettles's sharp voice rang out, giving Isabel a shock. "I hope that you were not about to jump that!" Ms. Nettles's glasses rattled on her bony nose as her unicorn halted.

"Of . . . of course not, Ms. Nettles," Isabel said quickly. "We were just making jumps, not jumping them."

"Definitely not jumping them," said Scarlett, shaking her head.

Ms. Nettles gave them a suspicious look. "You'd better be telling the truth, girls. You know the rules. First years are not allowed to jump without a teacher to supervise."

Thyme, her unicorn, nodded, his green-and-yellow tail swishing along with his head.

Scarlett swallowed back a giggle.

"It's for your own safety, so please abide by the rule. Now, it's almost dinnertime," Ms. Nettles continued. "Ride back to the stables with me."

"Yes, Ms. Nettles," the girls sighed.

Scarlett felt bad that Isabel hadn't gotten her turn at the jump. "Sorry," she mouthed.

"Next time," Isabel whispered back. They gave each other a thumbs-up behind the teacher's back. Scarlett felt a rush of happiness. She and Isabel had been friends since day one. They both loved riding fast and jumping high, although Isabel was much more competitive than Scarlett—she loved

to win, whereas Scarlett didn't care who won just as long as she was having fun.

The February sun was almost on the horizon as they neared the school building. The wintry rays lit up the magnificent pink-marble and colored-glass building, making it glow as if it were on fire.

"Unicorn Academy," Scarlett sighed happily. "It's so beautiful, especially now that it's snowing."

Her eyes moved from the grandness of the tall towers to the graceful curve of the domed roofs, then across the huge lawn to the multicolored lake with a tall fountain glittering at the center. The magical waters of Sparkle Lake flowed up from the center of the earth through the fountain, before rivers took it all over Unicorn Island. Every unicorn on the island drank its water every day to strengthen their magic and stay healthy.

"Unicorn Academy is the best school ever," agreed Isabel proudly. She shivered. "Brrrr, it's *soooo* cold. Look at the snowflakes landing on the lake. It must be freezing over."

"Imagine the fun we'll have if the lake does freeze," said Scarlett. "We can go ice skating."

Ms. Nettles's head whipped around. "Don't talk nonsense, girls! Sparkle Lake has never frozen over in the history of Unicorn Academy. It will take more than a cold snap to freeze its waters."

Isabel scrunched up her eyes against the low winter sun. "But it's so cold. Isn't there a tiny chance it could freeze?"

"It is unusually cold, I agree," said Ms. Nettles. "But I am sure the lake will withstand the temperature drop. If Sparkle Lake did freeze, it would mean the unicorns would be unable to drink the water they need, and that would be a disaster for the island. You would certainly not be allowed to ice skate! You're here to learn how to protect it—not to play on it! Now, stop chattering and take your unicorns into the stables and feed them. Be quick. If you're late for dinner, you shall clean my riding boots as punishment. Go on!"

As Ms. Nettles rode away toward the lake, Scarlett saw her pull a little bottle from her pocket, and the corners of the teacher's mouth turned up into a smile.

"What's she up to?" Scarlett wondered aloud. "She never smiles!"

"Who cares?" said Isabel. "How about a race?"

Scarlett immediately forgot about Ms. Nettles and grinned. "Why not! Last one back is a rotten egg!"

"It won't be us!" shouted Isabel. She and Cloud galloped full speed toward the stables.

"Go, Blaze!" Scarlett cried.

Blaze's breath spurted out clouds in the icy air as they gave chase, but they couldn't quite catch Cloud with her head start.

"We won!" said Isabel, punching the air in triumph. "Go, us!"

Scarlett didn't care. It had been a fun race even if Isabel had beaten her. "That was amazing," she said, sliding off and hugging Blaze. "Thank you, Blaze! You're the best unicorn here!"

Blaze nuzzled Scarlett back, her dark eyes shining happily.

Look for more adventures at Unicorn Academy!

PuRRmaids

Meet your newest feline friends!

PuRRmaids 1
The Scaredy Cat
Sudipta Bardhan-Qua

PuRRmaids 2
The Catfish Club
Sudipta Bardhan-Quallen

#1277

RHCBooks.com RHCB

Collect all the books in the Horse Diaries series!

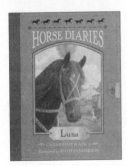

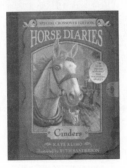

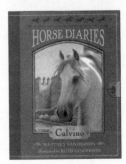